W9-ANB-231

Helping-Out Day?
Hooray!

W9-CNN-277

by Suzy Spafford

Level **1** Reader

READING LEVEL — PRE K–GRADE 1

11 12 13   NGS 10 9 8 7 6 5 4 3
CE13055/1011

Ms. O'Plume was a fun teacher!
Today she began class with a cheer:

"Let's pitch in and do some good.
And help our friends like we should.
Helping-Out Day! Hooooooray!
Now, let's all think.
How can we help others?"

"We can give away chocolate
chip cookies," said Emily.
"Think bigger," said Ms. O.
Emily tried again.
"How about *chocolate*
chocolate chip cookies?"

"We can clean up the park," Jack said.
"Or visit sick friends," said Corky.
"Excellent!" said Ms. O'Plume.

"Come up with more good ways
to help others," said Ms. O.
"Helping-Out Day is in one week!"

"Can we work together?" Suzy asked.
Ms. O smiled.
"That's what it's all about."

Suzy walked with her friends
after school.
They walked past Vivian's house.
"Oh, my!" said Suzy. "It's falling
apart. Why don't we fix it up for her?"

"That's a big job," said Corky.
"What can *we* do?"
 Jack said, "We can paint."
"And plant flowers,"
 added Emily.

"And hammer!" Suzy cried.
"My dad showed me how!"

"There is a lot of junk," said Corky.
"We can take it away," said Suzy,
"to the recycle place."

So the friends made a list
of everything they needed.
"I'll make lunch for us," said Emily.

The next day, Suzy showed
Ms. O'Plume how they would
fix Vivian's house.

"Great," said her teacher.
"But now you need to ask
Vivian if it's okay with her."

Suzy showed Vivian the plan.
Vivian did not look happy.
"Gee, thanks," said Vivian.
"But we like our house the way it is."

Suzy told her friends,
"Don't worry. She will like it.
She is just too shy to say it."

On Saturday,
the kids waited.
Once Vivian's
family went out...

they got to work!

Oops!
Jack spilled paint on Corky.
"That's okay!" Suzy laughed.
"Green is your color!"

They were almost done!
The friends looked at the house.

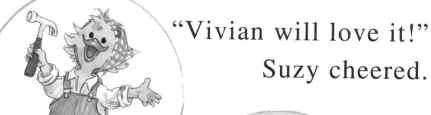
"Vivian will love it!"
Suzy cheered.

But when
Vivian came home. . .

"Oh, no!" Vivian cried.
"My house! My yard!"
"You don't like it?" Suzy asked.
"Well," said Vivian,
"we warthogs like. . ."

"Roses?" tried Suzy.
"More flowers?"

Snortwood's
Junkyard

"No. More junk!" Vivian said.
"We Snortwoods run the town junkyard."

The next day. . .

Suzy's class went to an art show.

Suzy loved to go see new things. . .

. . .but today she did not look around.
She did not feel happy.
Helping-Out Day did not go well.

"I did not listen to Vivian,"
she said sadly.

"What is *that*?" Emily asked.
"A new kind of art," said Ms. O'Plume.
"Isn't it *pretty*?" said Vivian.
"It is art from the heart!"

"I could make that!" said Jack.

Suzy smiled.

"Maybe we *all* could!" she said.

The next day, Suzy and her friends
took all the junk back to the
Snortwood's yard.
(Vivian said it was okay, of course!)
They made an art show of their own.

Vivian was very happy!
"This is perfect for us!" she cried.

"Very good job!" said Ms. O'Plume.
"I *love* the tree made of old cans!"

Everyone came to see
Snortwood's Junkyard.
"It's amazing!" said some.
"It's great!" said others.
"It's recycled!" Ms. O told them.

SNORTWOOD'S
JUNKYARD

"Thank you," said Vivian.
"Here are presents for you."
And they were very nice presents—
because they came from the heart.